Animal Dreaming

AN ABORIGINAL DREAMTIME STORY

by Paul Morin

STODDART KIDS

To Alfred with thanks,
and for Janine, with whom I share my time and space

The author gratefully acknowledges
the assistance of the Australian High Commission
for its help in researching.

We acknowledge the Canada Council for the Arts and the Ontario Arts Council
for their support of our publishing program.

Published in Canada in 1998 by Stoddart Kids,
a division of Stoddart Publishing Co. Limited
34 Lesmill Road
Toronto, Canada M3B 2T6
Tel (416)445-3333 Fax (416)445-5967
e-mail Customer.Service@ccmailgw.genpub.com

Published in the United States of America by Silver Whistle,
a trademark of Harcourt Brace & Company

Canadian Cataloguing in Publication Data
Morin, Paul, 1959-
Animal dreaming: an aboriginal story
ISBN 0-7737-3062-1
1. Australian aborigines - Folklore - Juvenile literature.
2. Legends - Australia - Juvenile literature. I. Title
PS8576.0667A75 1998   j398.2'099915   C97-931718-5   PZ8.1.M8255An 1998

Some of the paintings in this book were done in alkyds on canvas,
while the Dreamtime images were done in acrylics on wood;
these works were influenced by traditional Dreamtime images.
The text type was set in Cloister Old Style.
The display type was set in OptiFantastik.
Color separations by Tien Wah Press, Singapore
Printed and bound by Tien Wah Press, Singapore
This book was printed on totally chlorine-free Nymolla Matte Art paper.
Production supervision by Stanley Redfern
Designed by Lisa Peters

THE AUSTRALIAN ABORIGINES believe that long, long ago the earth was soft and had no form. The features of the landscape were created as the result of the heroic acts of ancestral spirits, who often assumed the form of animals. The origins of land shapes—mountains, deserts, and water holes—echo these events, which the Aborigines refer to as Dreamtime. For at least fifty thousand years, the Aborigines have maintained the traditions of Dreamtime through stories, music, dance, art, and ceremony. And in the land around Kakadu, this tradition is honored today.

In May 1996, I had an opportunity to explore Arnhem Land and Kakadu National Park, in the Northern Territories of Australia. During this time I met with Bill Neidjie, a Gagadju elder. Bill continues to teach the stories of Dreamtime to all who will listen. I spent memorable hours with him in and around the East Alligator River and Cannon Hill, the sacred place of his Dreaming. He spoke with deep sadness about the loss of respect toward ceremony and the Dreamtime. I am grateful to him for sharing his time and stories with me.

Some Australian Words Used in This Book

Bal-an-ga one of the ancestor beings, a long-necked turtle

bandicoot a small mammal

Din-e-wan one of the ancestor beings, an emu

dingo the wild dog of Australia

Dreamtime the eternity of creation, spanning from the beginning of time through the present and future

Gagadju a tribe from the northern territory of Australia

Garn-dag-itj one of the ancestor beings, a kangaroo

Kip-a-ara name for the initiation ceremonies at which boys learned the ways of manhood

kookaburra a bird in the kingfisher family

Na-marr-gon the lightning god

outback a remote part of the bush

walkabout a journey, either alone or in a group

ON A LAND called Australia, in the moment just before dawn, a boy and man waited for the light of the last stars to fade from the sky.

Mirri climbed to his favorite perch in the tree. All night long he had not been able to sleep. Today was Kip-a-ara, the time Gadurra, Mirri's friend and elder, would take him into the outback and tell him about the time when the earth was first shaped. Today was the day of Animal Dreaming.

"Today we will visit the sacred places of our people, and tomorrow you will learn the stories about our beginnings, the Animal Dreaming," Gadurra said in his deep voice.

In the light of the new day, the two set off on walkabout to the howl of dingoes and the sound of their own footsteps. As they walked

into the outback, Gadurra pointed out special water holes, rocks, and trees, and told their stories. "This is the home of Na-marr-gon, the Lightning Man," said Gadurra as they came upon a rock outcrop. "It is he who brings the thunder and rain. Our people believe the rocks and wind are alive, and you can hear them if you listen."

At day's end they stopped, and Gadurra pointed out the rock
paintings on the stones surrounding their campsite. Gadurra began.
"Sit quietly, my friend, and see what the paintings tell you." Mirri
and Gadurra talked on as the light faded, and then the two slept.

At sunrise Mirri awoke to the sharp sound of clapping sticks and the elder's singing. When Mirri gazed up at the animals painted on the rock walls, they seemed almost alive.

Gadurra spoke.

LONG AGO, at the beginning of the Dreamtime, War-ra-mur-run-gun-di, the Great Ancestor, gave life to the four-leggeds, and the winged and the gilled ones. All lived together in the same watery place. Some swam, while others splashed at the water's edge. Life was bountiful and all was well.

But then Mau-ri-woo-ti, the white-breasted Sea Eagle, grew to believe he should rule, as master of the wetlands. Next, Koo-ka-bur-ra, the laughing Kingfisher, decided that it should be the birds who ruled over all. Because they were greedy, Pelican and Egret quickly agreed.

All the birds wanted the land for themselves.

Soon birds from wide and far gathered together in hundreds, and then in thousands, until the land grew dark in their shadow. With sharp beaks and outstretched talons, they attacked the land from above.

The fish, animals, and reptiles cried out for help. Soon came the thunderous sound of animals of every sort rushing to their rescue from the four directions. Out of the mudflats came Gin-ga, the Crocodile, and Al-mudj, the Rainbow Serpent. There were Band-i-coots from the grasslands and Wombats from the rainforest. Gun-da-men, the Frilled Lizard, came from the desert. All joined in the battle. Still the birds fought with all their might.

But there were three who would not fight. Garn-dag-itj, the Ancestral Kangaroo, Bal-an-ga, the Ancestral Long-Necked Turtle, and Din-e-wan, the Ancestral Emu. Instead, they went off and talked of how they may bring peace to the earth.

They came here to this place. They danced and sang as the moon and stars lit their way. Each one had a dream.

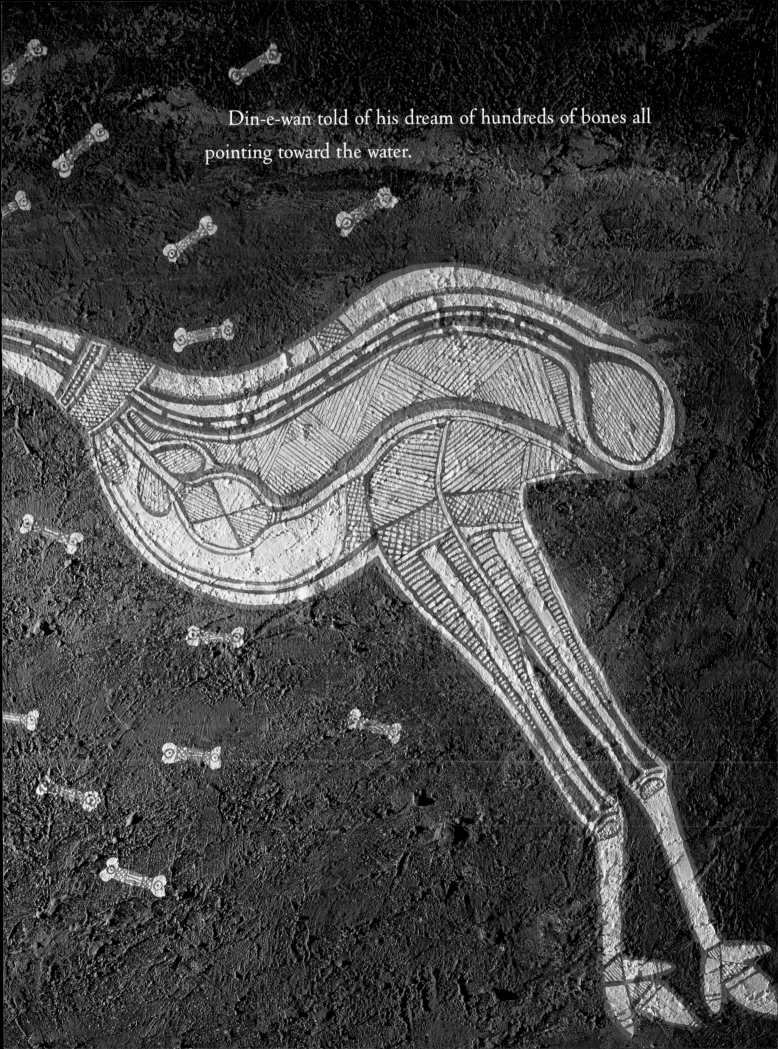

Din-e-wan told of his dream of hundreds of bones all pointing toward the water.

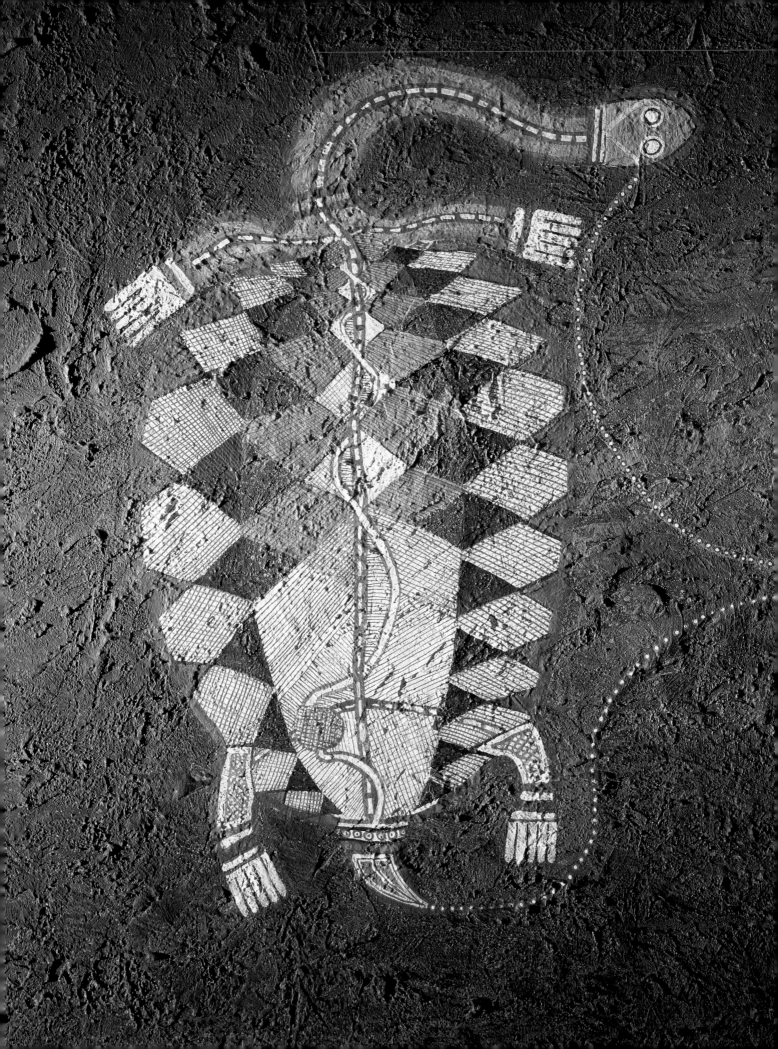

In his dreaming, Bal-an-ga had seen an enormous wave wash over
the earth.

Garn-dag-itj had dreamed of a digging bone.

Upon wakening, she reached inside her pouch and found that bone. When she stabbed the earth with it, of its own power the bone began to move toward the water, digging as it went.

Soon the land was torn by a deep channel, and thunder filled the air. A moment later, a huge tidal wave came up from behind the cliff where the three stayed for safety.

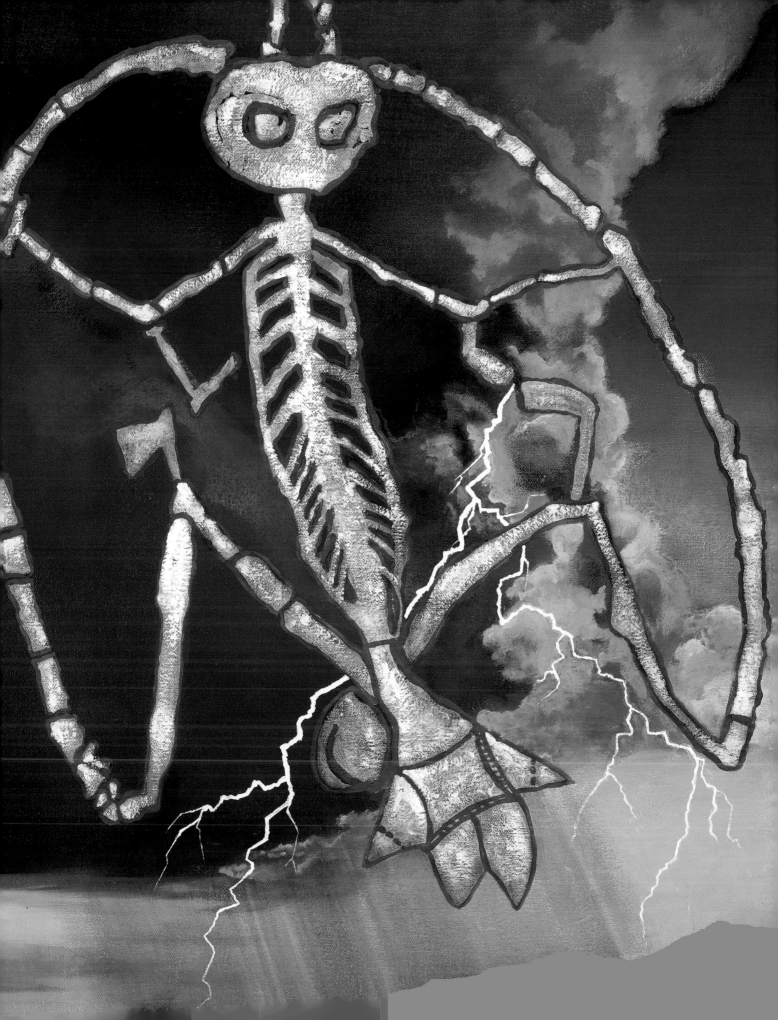

A strange light flickered in the air as the surging water settled. Gin-ga, the Crocodile, turned himself to stone, and his bumps became part of the landscape. Snakes, using their powerful coils, made hills and great stone archways. Bar-ra-mun-di, the Great Fish, created large water holes in which to swim. Deep mangrove swamps gave shadows to the night. Even the birds painted feathered clouds across the sky.

Before long, each of the animals had made their home in the land. The animals were at peace.

And from that day on, when they dreamed, they lived their dreams.

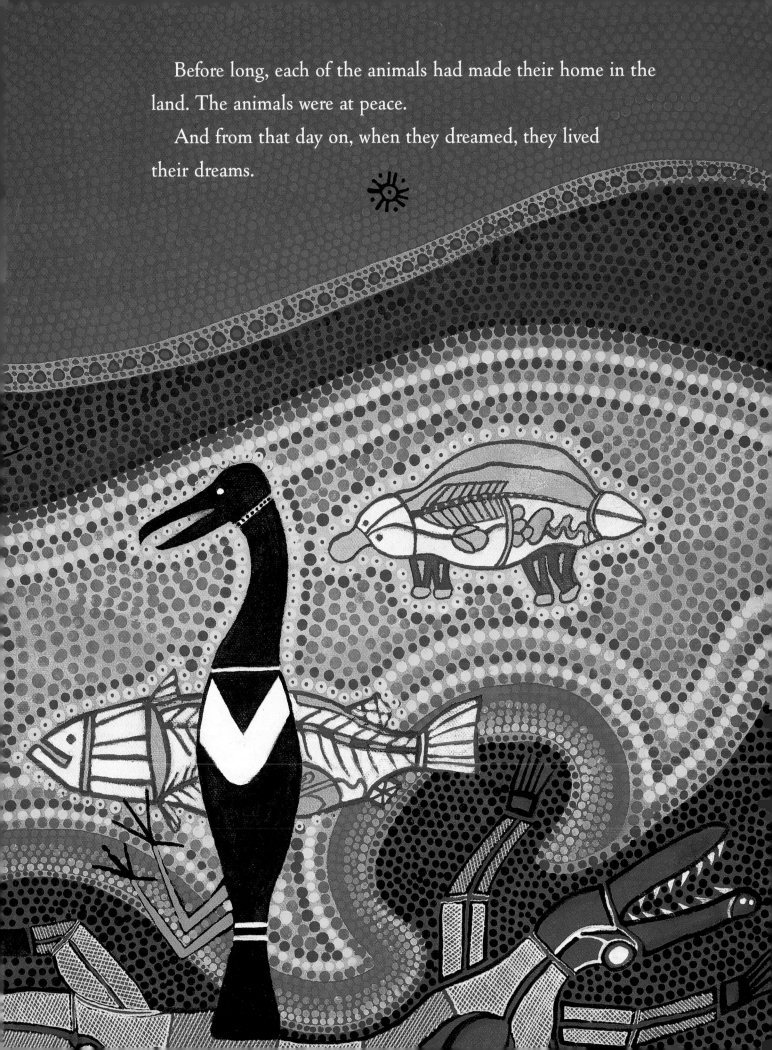

Mirri watched as Gadurra then traced his hand across the rock. "These paintings contain the story of Dreamtime. We keep the Dreaming alive by listening, passing on our story, and by leaving our mark on this rock."

Mirri understood, but knew it was time to return home.

Someday, he knew, his own time would come to leave his mark here.

Animal dreaming.